SNARL

JOHN BODEN

DEAD SKY PUBLISHING

Published by Dead Sky Publishing, LLC
Miami Beach, Florida

Cover by Chad Lutzke

Edited by Anna Kubik
Copyedited by Kristy Baptist

ISBN 9781639510856 (paperback)
ISBN 9781639511037 (ebook)

First U.S. Edition September 2023

Praise for John Boden

"The characters in John Boden's Snarl speak with a dark poetry which comes naturally to rural people accustomed to chronic ailments, gossip, and disaster. It manages that trick of being both moving and beautifully horrific." — **Steve Rasnic Tem,** author of *The Night Doctor And Other Tales, Deadfall Hotel* and *Thana Trauma*

"A study in grief and need, in desire and inertia, in the power and prison of love, Snarl is a symphony of melancholia. Try to get through this one with your heart intact, I dare you." — **Alan Baxter,** author of *Devouring Dark, Sallow End* and *The Gulp*

"John Boden's Snarl is a combination of knockout-punch prose, touching storytelling and a strong dose of what-the-hell. It's the author at his best." — **Sam W. Anderson,** author of *The Sentimental Assassin, The Nines* and *Slightly Off Center*

"John Boden writes a world full of colorful and vibrant characters. His voice is special, unique and marvelous. Snarl is a story full of emotions—sadness and longing, fear and love, converging into a powerful conclusion. Every page of this story had me eager to read the next." — **Mark Matthews,** author of *The Hobgoblin of Little Minds, Body Of Christ* and *Milk-Blood*

"Fantastic rural noir with a dash of dark fantasy and a tear-inducing end only Boden could create." — **Chad Lutzke,** author of *Cannibal Creator, The Neon Owl* and *Of Foster Homes & Flies*

"Snarl broke me into tiny pieces. Boden's voice is strong, sincere and utterly unique. This is a love letter to all the great country songs of your life, lyrical and heartaching. I was literally speechless when I finished." — **Robert Ford,** author of *Burner, Inner Demons* and *Blood Rose*

"There's a level of wordsmithing happening with John that is unparalleled. Images that are shocking and beautiful, and you see the way he has arranged his words and they are these intricate configurations that are just....wow." — **Kristi DeMeester,** author of *Beneath* and *Such A Pretty Smile*

"His luggage was the bags beneath his eyes"
— Ron Young, LITTLE CAESAR, "Ridin' On" from the album, *Influence*

"I never let nothing be as easy as that."
— Joe Henry, "Beautiful Hat" from the album, *Fuse*

"Someone once said to me that if you want to make God laugh, just tell him your plans. Just tell him who you are."
— Jack Ketchum, *Peaceable Kingdom*

— 1 —

Notebook #2, page 33:

That funky new thing that pulled itself from the mire, that swam up from darker depths, growing and twisting and changing. The thing that pulled itself from the wet, gasping, and terrified in the dirty sand. That walked on land and kept evolving. That sorry thing was time. And no greater monster had ever been loosed… Until doubt crawled ashore, sometime after.

— 2 —

June 1998

Marlin Stains held the tiny stub of a pencil between his thumb and forefinger, tight enough that all color had blanched from the flesh. His wrist had begun to go all pins-and-needles from resting against the edge of the desk for so long. He bared his teeth as he wrung out one last thought, a sentence fragment dripping onto the page. Like blood.

Like a promise or one's word, time is, indeed, the poorest currency.

The tilt of his cursive on the faded lines of the old notebook page was a comforting kiss to his jangled nerves. Some days, getting home to his notebooks and pencil was the only balm he was afforded. He felt safe in his room. A secure vault where nearly every shelf and surface was taken over by paper, bound, clipped, or stapled, soldiers numbering hundreds, to hold his words safe and guard him.

***

"Getting it out of your head and onto paper is sometimes the best way for getting on…"Old Mr. Wish spoke those words in a voice that was barnwood, as he fed handfuls of scribbled pages into the burning barrel at the edge of his yard. Words eagerly devoured by flame and offered back to the heavens as reverse manna. He stood and read a few more pages before tossing them into the fire, dry lips moving as he did so. His eyes took on a dour cast, and he sniffed hard and dropped the entire handful of papers into the mouth of the barrel. There was a crackling sound as the flames chewed his words, long ago tattooed on paper to cinders. Fire has teeth that snap.

The next day, Marlin bought his first notebook. A thin thing with a yellow cover that cost a pair of quarters. Fifty pages of white paper lined blue. Over the years, that one had blossomed into a myriad. Filled with fragments of prose, wordplay and story, parable, and poem. Every word was a cell that made up Marlin Stains. Made up a secret Marlin Stains the world was not allowed to see. Not a one ever seen or read by another, and still yet to be introduced to match or flame.

— 3 —

Marlin had asked his mother the question, six years earlier.

He was younger, but years past being draped over that line between boy and man. He had returned from a visit with his dying father. It had only been a month prior the doctor told them he was being eaten from the inside out. Dr. Whitten had seemed surprised the family had not been in the know, as Mason Stains had gotten his diagnosis almost half a year earlier. But Mason liked to carry weight and what could be heavier and more personal than one's own demise. The man was champion at Sisyphus-ing that shit until he could no longer do so, and he just dropped his aching arms and let that boulder roll.

Marlin came into the trailer and sat down, late breeze silent and just as weak. He had been home for nearly twenty minutes before his mother emerged from the hall and noticed him.

"How was that?"

The small woman asked. A question that was more habitual courtesy than functional inquiry often asked after a funeral or a root canal, where the best answer is really not to answer at all. Marlin looked at her with tired blue eyes that always seemed ready to shed water.

Marlin took off his hat and dropped it on the floor by his feet. He paid no mind to the cat that appeared to sniff at the sweaty fabric.

"It was fine…as far as watching the man who sired you… then left you…then wanted to be part of your life again, watching that man evaporate a visit at a time." Marlin frowned, trying to not let his anger at the circumstances boil over onto his well-meaning mother. "It's like a photograph fading before your very eyes. Like someone erases the picture real slow…"

The older woman nodded; her lips formed a curt line. Her eyes held all the compassion he'd ever wanted or needed. "I know," she muttered. Tall minutes of silence circled them like buzzards.

"I hate this." Marlin's voice was a gavel bang. "I hate that I can't even be easily wrecked by my father dying…it has to be as complicated as everything else. Rooms full of selfish envy and sadness, dishonesty is so rich in our veins…" He trailed off and whimpered under his breath.

"My, you do have a way with words." The woman smiled wanly and then licked her lips before continuing on. "I once read where a human is just a dollar's worth of chemicals and water. I think when I first heard this fact it was eighty-nine cents worth so I'm allowing for inflation. But I've known people who seemed to be worth so much more and I've known others I wouldn't waste on a ragweed garden. People are people, Son. Stupid animals, yet they are also all the gods and devils. They are shadow boxes that only flicker the image we give the candle for. You've a right to be angry and hurting. You are losing something you've only recently gotten back…"

Her bony hand on his shoulder was a millstone.

"Was my father a good man?"

Her eyes narrowed and the breath she took in through her nose was an audible hiss, she reached over to the cluttered table by the chair and fished a smoke from the pack, lit it, and perched it on her lip. She sucked in the smoke and held it prisoner for a long minute. When she spoke, the words made a wizard's entrance through the cancerous mist.

"He was. When we first met…he was the nicest man. A beautiful man. A kind man." She stared at the wall and kept her eyes from his for the duration of her speaking.

"One time, early on, we was talking…I loved listening to that man talk. Stories of his growing up poor with all his brothers and sisters. Their adventures. Life on the mountain. He had such a reverence and that rich voice. Filled you up like fresh bread."

Another deep drag. The room had grown so quiet, he could hear the small crinkling sound of shredded tobacco burning in its paper chrysalis, to be reborn in seconds as silvery smoke.

"I told your father that I had grown up near the lake but had never been on it. Oh, I'd swum in it countless times but had never taken a boat out on it. Never been further than maybe twenty feet from shore. So, one weekend, he picked me up. We was still dating, mostly to the movies or the diner, and I asked what we were doing, and he ignored me. Just sat there driving with a stupid half-smile on his face. I started getting mad, as can be my way, and badgered him the whole drive. When he parked by the edge of the lake and we got out, he took my hand. We walked to the edge of the water. It lapped the small, pebbled beach loudly and smelled divine, like years. I could smell time in it. Ancient creatures that swirled beneath its surface eons ago. I closed my eyes and saw schools of white fish swimming that had long ago been digested in the bellies of the natives 'round here."

She stopped talking and smoked another cigarette to nothing.

Marlin winced.

"I know you're afraid of water. Scared of boats, Hell, you used to cry when it'd rain too long." she chuckled and after lighting a third cigarette, continued.

"Your father had gotten a boat, nothing much, just a simple aluminum fishing boat, one of them squarish ones, probably his brother Jim's, and he told me he was going to take me out on the lake. We would drift under the stars for the first time. He helped me in and pushed it out before he jumped in himself. He rowed us out nearer the center of the lake. The few buildings on the shore looked like toys, like them little cardboard houses that come with train sets. I looked over the side and the water was just glistening black. As we stilled and the small waves slowed. The water calmed. It looked like a mirror. We were sitting in the middle of a giant mirror. I looked at your dad and he was smiling, and I think I was crying. I said, "Oh, it's so beautiful." He laughed. What a laugh that man had…and he says to me, 'Look up then down', so I did. Marlin, there were so many stars that night. The sky was crammed full and when I looked up at them and then down at the black water, the stars were reflected there as clear and well. It was like we were floating in space."

The old woman was crying then, quietly, and tears had streaked her cheeks, blooming them ruddy. She sniffled and stubbed out her smoke. "Next to you, that was the best thing he ever gave me."

"And Merle?" Marlin whispered but the woman did not hear or gave no indication to acknowledge if she had. The muslin smile that flitted to her lips to be gone just as quick could have meant anything.

Marlin nodded and leaned back in the chair. He closed his eyes and tried to recall any moment in his childhood not marred by longing or guilt or regret. Zero is an easy number to count to.

"You asked me if your dad was a good man…I think most wicked men see a good man's face in the mirror. Least I 'spect that's what they reckon to themselves…I'd not say he was ever truly wicked; I don't think he ever done any of the things he did to purposefully hurt another. He was selfish. He'd grown up having to share everything and when he was grown, he wanted to have it all to himself. We all are or can be. Your father just had no truck to say no, especially when it came to saying it to himself. I don't think he ever even saw the things he did as bad or hurtful…just what he wanted." Her dark lips lifted, parted, allowed more words to tumble out.

"Nothing stronger than the lies we tell ourselves. How's that old saying go…If hope was enough and wishes were sins, I can't remember…"

She trailed off and her eyes, small pools of brown shine clouded, and moisture escaped to run down her hollow cheeks.

"But I can tell you one undeniable truth, you're a good man, Son."

"It's all I aim for, I guess." Marlin stood and kicked off his boots. "I'm going to have a shower and head for bed. Being is tiresome." He stomped back down the hallway before she had even looked in his direction.

"Being what?"

"Just being," and then he was just footsteps on the thin carpet.

"Ok, goodnight, Son." She plucked one more cigarette

from the pack and smoked in the plain glow of the television, where a muted Tom Selleck chased a man on a beach.

— 4 —

2001, one week from the end of June

Marlin counted the bobbing bright of the fireflies, the thick grass beneath them whispering in the evening breeze.

Some summers, there were barely any to note, then there were others, like this one, where the bouncing dots of luminescence seemed downright otherworldly in number. The fairy magic of fantasy movies and Disney cartoons.

Marlin Stains sat on the bowing wooden steps that led to the front porch of the trailer, a bottle of soda in a slender hand. Condensation dripped onto the gravel at his feet, darkening it to a deep slate. The last fingers of the sun were pulling over the mountain, with the sky darkening in its slow chase. Dusk always seemed like a gasp from tired lungs, He thought.

Marlin squinted at the house across the road. It crouched where it had as long as he could remember, its unlighted windows were black mouths that hung open, yet spoke not at all. The porch roof sagged, and a few rotten boards hung from the awning like ribs. Marlin drank the last of his cola and dropped the bottle in the crate by the steps. The clink echoed across the quiet evening.

Mr. Wish, or Aloysius Wesley Garman, as he was christened at birth, had been in the ground nearly a dozen years, but if Marlin closed his tired eyes, he could still see the old man. Sitting in his rusted folding chair at the back edge of the driveway, smoking a seemingly endless stream of Pall Malls. He could almost hear the water slosh in the old bucket that sat by the old man's feet, the one that held his beer in melting ice. He could hear the gunshot of the tab being pulled and the slurp of foam as Mr. Wish sucked down that first gulp. He closed his eyes and listened to the bats squeaking as they dove for mosquitoes and biting flies. It took seconds for even that slight sampler of sounds to solidify into firmer memories.

"You ever done a thing that you regretted, son?" The old man's words rode on the smoke that fled his mouth. Marlin thought of bluish phantoms escaping a gaping cavern. Wish's large fingers looked like ginger root as they held the smoking butt between them.

"Once." The boy shuffled his gaze along with his feet, though he remained in place. His voice was very small in the big night.

In the feeble reach of the porch light, Mr. Wish looked positively ancient. Wrinkles upon wrinkles formed run-on sentences, punctuated with liver spots and moles. He brought the small stub of a cigarette to his nearly toothless mouth and sucked so hard; the end screamed red like a wound. He squinted at Marlin as the smoke leaked from nostrils and lips.

"Once ain't never been fed, Boy."

He let that hang like tallow for a moment before throwing more sticky words at it.

"Once is a hungry thing. But if's you feed it, it'll grow to twice…then that to three times and before you know it you done grown up a bad fuckin' habit." He flicked the dead cigarette to the ground where it joined dozens of others. He pulled the crumpled red pack from his shirt pocket and had another nesting on his lip almost instantaneously, like a magic trick. The lighter chinked and the slight breeze carried the metallic ozone smell of the fluid to the boy's nostrils.

Marlin listened and found his gaze not stuck to the old man, but the air above him, as though his scalding words flew about him like a swarm of gnats awaiting the hungry mouths of bats.

"Well, boy…what was it you done?"

Mr. Wish showed his few teeth when he asked it, the few he had were crooked and gray like old cemetery stones.

"I killed my brother…"

"Like Cain?" The old man said it as though the words were wrapped in chain too heavy to quite spit out.

"I don't know. I'm not sure who that is."

"The Bible, son."

"We don't have one."

The old man's features bled shadowy, and a sad expression moved over his face before he spoke again.

"Our father's who that bastard was…every one of us came from that sorrowful line. Every damned one of us, sired from greed and jealousy, to be prammed with a heartful of violence. Can't never wash them sheets clean." At that, the man laughed, and it was dry stones being rubbed together, followed by meaty coughing…clunking…

Marlin opened his eyes at the sound of Miss Maggie's ancient truck rattling past on the valley road and stayed on the steps watching until her taillights disappeared in the shadows. He stood and went inside the trailer where his mother was dying, a minute at a time.

— 5 —

Notebook #12, page 14, in top margin, red ink:
Sometimes, missing a thing you've never really known is as painful as losing a loved one. That void being an emotional phantom

limb syndrome of sorts, a small feeling of absence that lightly pinches the backs of your subconscious legs, leaving invisible welts that sting like jellyfish kisses.

— 6 —

Daily

Marlin knew the feeling well and good had been close to going steady with it since the day he was born. You know nothing but guilt when you're born with blood on your hands. When the first thing you've done, as soon as you had enough cells to do it, was strangle your brother in the womb. The very cord that provided your nourishment being the noose that choked the life from your cellmate sibling.

Marlin sat on the toilet and stared at his tired face in the dirty mirror above the sink. Only in his dawning thirties, he saw an old man through the haze of toothpaste-spit-stain-spatter and water spots. The small sections they obscured seemed a blessing to him. He refocused his gaze on the faucet, on the dripping water and the constant *blip* when it hit the porcelain. He found his brain wondering, for the millionth time in his thirty-two years, to what his brother might have become.

A doctor? A dealer? A lawyer? A bricklayer? A reprobate?

He cleaned himself and stood, not bothering to flush or pull up his pants just yet. He heard the phone ringing in the other room. Heard the small stomps of his mother's slippered feet.

What if it was you that had died in Mama's womb?

What if Merle was born and all this time you've been a ghost haunting his life? Would it be all that different?

Still be swaddled in chains either way, right?

Marlin pushed the commode handle, stepping back to the sink to brush his teeth. He had to get to work as he made his way out the door, he saw the note on the counter beneath his keys.

Lisa called, was all it said.

— 7 —

Tip top of July

Marlin looked at her as she dozed. The husk that she had become reminded him of when he was small. Of the locust shells he collected from the trunks of trees out at Pap's farm, terrifying and fragile, yet tenaciously clinging on. He used to call them hard ghosts and kept them in an old Band-Aid tin. He smiled slightly at the realization that he still collected ghosts. Mama lay sunken in the recliner, a mummy shrouded in crocheted afghans and flannel. A cat on her lap, eyes closed as her skeletal fingers scratched his ears, a mechanical action even in sleep. Cigarettes had been banned from the trailer for over a year now, but the smell still clung with talons. It was oddly comforting.

The thought of picture day in the second grade bubbled up for some reason. Marlin closed his eyes and breathed deep. Watching his twenty-four years ago self-walking down the street to the store to fetch her smokes, never realizing he was an accessory to her current condition. Not quite murder, but he couldn't help but feel the erosion of her lungs and liver bore his sooty fingerprints. Room was something that there always seemed to be plenty of in his guilt locker.

He bit the tip of his tongue until it bled and sniffed back the scald of tears that were summoned. *Sometimes to know you're well, something must come along and hurt you,* he had once read. He wondered if there was an inverse to that adage. *When all you've ever had was hurt, would you even know well if it bit you on the ass?*

He screwed on a smile and stepped into the room from the shadows of the kitchen, wearing the costume of the wellest man there ever was.

"Hello, Mama."

He leaned down and slipped his arms around the frail creature who bore him. She snaked a hand up to his neck. Her breath smelled like a wound as he leaned down, kissed her dry cheek. There was joy in her weary eyes.

"So happy to see you, honey." A voice as thin as dragonfly wings. She smiled, showing pale gums and loose teeth, and weakly pointed to the couch. Marlin sat down and another cat bolted from beneath the sofa. A blur of black fur that disappeared into the shadows of the hallway.

"Callie cat never was able to warm up to people." His mother's voice was tired. Tired enough for a dozen folks.

"It's okay. I'm the same way." Marlin tried to smile when he replied, but they never seemed to fit right on him.

"You get that honestly, Son. Hell of an inheritance. Don't spend it all at once." The brittle woman chuckled, but it grew into a fit of ragged coughing that lasted the longest minute. She quelled the fit and smiled apologetically as her breathing returned to its regular slow rasp. From back the hall, Tommy Cat had emerged. Looking annoyed or stoned but just quite old.

"How was work?"

"It was," he answered, and reached a hand down to allow the ancient yellow cat to sniff at his fingertips.

"Work is called work for a reason, if it were pleasant, it'd be called something different. Something nicer rather than like something you cough up."

"Did the hospital lady call today? She was to call about bringing the tank and setting up your oxygen." Marlin tried to sound buoyant when he asked, but just saying the words caused his insides to drop. It was a step. A step in a direction he knew well.

"She did. Around two, I believe. She asked again about if we had considered hospice. I was watching Magnum. I love his mustache."

"And?"

"What, he was a cutie."

"No, about the tank…and the hospice nurse?"

"Oh, she'll be by on Thursday around three to get it set up, I told her I'd see if you could come home early to talk to her, I won't remember nothin' she says. I don't want a stranger fussin' over me while I die. I slid into the world fanfare free, I wanna go out the same. I take their damn pain meds and the other pills and gunk they want me to swallow. And all it's doing is what, slowing the slide. making me sleep so I don't have to listen to the teeth chewing me up inside, feel 'em grinding me to nil? Well, when I hit the end I wanna slide out on my own terms. No strangers, just us." She paused a moment and tilted her look down at the floor so as to not meet her son's moist gaze.

"And I'd prefer that slippage to occur while you are at work. I couldn't bear to do that to you." Her skeletal hand squeezed his arm and it hurt, but he made himself smile anyway. The amount of pain she was enduring, the nurse had admitted, had to be close to unfathomable.

"I can do that. And I'll tell her your wishes on the other." He danced over the landmines she'd just scattered.

Marlin nodded and watched her close her eyes. Watched

her small smile dissolve to a thin line, and when her small snores flitted around like evening moths, he cried as quietly as he could.

When that passed, he stood and watched his dear mother sleep in the flickering glow of the small, muted television, the volume turned so low it sounded like a conscience.

— 8 —

Composition Book #21, Page 9, Faded pencil:
The greatest toil is the one of self, the sanest you aching and arching to strangle the unhinged you; this action akin to trying to fight one's reflection in a mirror. Difference being that in time, a person can tear themselves in two and suffer twice the agonies as each part of them bleeds to death.

Another word for this is harmony, which we all know is the sharpest knife in the drawer.

— 9 —

July, eleven days in
The truck was warm, even with the driver's side window down a little. It was broken and always partly down. Rain, snow, sleet, and sun, it would be hanging slightly open like an idiot's mouth.

The sun was gone for the day, leaving a sky that was cavity-in-a-molar dark. Marlin took another gulp from the can of flat soda and sat it back on the dashboard. A small puddle now resided there, the sum of a bad barter between a cold can and the humid summer air. He closed his eyes and breathed in deeply. The smoke from the Viceroy dying in the ashtray flowed around him like spectral fingers. The smell made him think of his father. That had been his brand. Marlin had never smoked, never even tried it, but somehow after his dad had died, he'd found that the smell of a Viceroy burning away seemed to calm him. He glanced out of the corner of his eye and could almost see the older man in the passenger seat. Carved from soft smoke like some ancient pictograph etched in cool stone. A photo in silver x-ray.

He smiled and reckoned he could hear his father's rough voice in his head, as it helped him internally talk through whatever things were eating him. And there was always something eating him.

Marlin was practically a smorgasbord.

He tipped a finger to his lips and worked at the sliver of skin by the nail with his slightly crooked teeth. Pulled at it until he tasted blood. He spat the hangnail on the floor, wiped his bleeding fingertip on his jeans, but within seconds, started chewing another finger's flesh.

"Never could leave well enough alone."

He looked over to the empty seat beside him and smirked.

"That's my thing, Dad. Only thing I ever been good at."

"You've been good at plenty, you just never let any of it outta your head or your heart. You got notebooks full of what you're good at."

"Well, all that stuff is starting to boil. I feel like a pressure cooker about to explode. All my stillborn dreams have lain rotten for so long… I'm like wet hay in a closed-up barn."

"Sometimes burning is the most glorious escape."

"I have no reason, Dad. No reason to be this angry. Sad, yes, and maybe a bit mad at the fact that all I get to chew on are unhappy bones. I feel like I'm going mad."

"I've never known a madman who didn't have a reason or a cause."

"I've had both, as well as good intentions, but all my good intentions ate their own." Marlin mumbled as he grabbed the butt from the ashtray. He crushed it out against dirty metal.

"And this one time, I think I may be able to make a difference."

In the barren excuse for a yard across the street, a dog barked.

A door opened.

A voice hollered, "Shut the fuck up!"

Marlin finished his warm drink and dropped the can behind the seat. He closed his eyes so tightly that they stung when he opened them again.

A light went on in the modular he was watching, bright as a smoker's smile. He looked at the claw hammer on the console beside him, and at the thought of holding it in his hand, a light went out in his heart.

— 10 —

Early June 2001

Joe Waller sat at the end of the bar; on the same stool he had claimed nearly a decade ago. *His* spot. The end of the bar, nearest the corridor that led back to the restrooms. The vinyl covering of the stool was ripped then taped together with red duct tape, making it stand out in sharp contrast to the rest of the stools that lined the bar. It had survived two redecorations, a small fire, and nearly half a dozen brawls. It had kissed many bottoms and the occasional drunken forehead. It was Joe's, and Mike the owner made sure it was always there for him, like a true friend.

He looked at his knuckles through the haze of Marlboro smoke, the fog that was coming after his sixth beer adding to the murk. They were still swollen angry red, the middle one hosting a small slit scabbed with a dark ruby. He slung back the last of the beer and grimaced. At home, Lisa would be nursing her wounds with a dish towel full of ice, shedding not-so-quiet tears. He looked closer at the broken skin of his knuckle and wondered if he'd chipped her tooth. His lips became a thin line as he tapped two fingers on the bar, and within seconds, Mike materialized to refill the glass.

"You good, Joe? You look like you've been through it."

"I was born through it. But, yeah, I'll be okay." Joe nodded as he sipped the fresh beer, "I'm what they call a survivor." The smile he forced fit like sun-dried leather. It almost creaked. Mike nodded before he once again vanished like a phantom.

Joe hated what he'd become. He had been raised better.

Never put your hands on a woman, never.

They were words he'd heard from his father and grandpa, as well as any man he'd ever been fortunate enough to gather advice from. He tilted his head, making his neck pop audibly. Lisa was a good woman, mostly. She was smart, strong, and pretty. She adored him, really adored his money and the ease it brought to their lives. She had never strayed or questioned a thing he asked of her. She gave him a beautiful daughter, grown and away at already-paid-for college, and they had created a son that never made it beyond a suck of wet wheezing breath in the delivery room.

He had loved her with all his heart. Then one day he realized what a yoke his life had become. He was forty-seven and shackled to a boulder. A boulder that looked like his wife and daughter. He worked all week and worked at his family in the time that remained, but he felt as though he was drowning. And doesn't fear often beget anger, and doesn't anger pal around with violence? Yeah, he felt like he was sinking.

His lifeboat was Leeny, the desk girl at the salvage yard. She was nice, and always accommodating with a kind word, an eyeful of tit or some other flirtatious invitation. The first time they slept together was the night of Lisa's birthday. He was three hours late getting home and hadn't even bothered with a card or an apology.

His other cracks began to show soon after. But money was often the best bandage, he also discovered.

There were times when Lisa-would do things, sometimes just small things, often next to nothing--but sometimes, he was sure she knew what she was fishing for. Knew just how to dangle the line to get his bite and then his mind would go to white out. Like his thoughts were a radio turned down soft only to have a sudden blare of static kill the calm. When that happened, he stepped out of himself and another stepped in. That other was not a man of patience or kindness but one of punch and holler. Of blame, bitterness, and guilt. Of selfishness and need. When the tears dried and the bruises healed, he'd offer an apology and an open checkbook and life put on its boogie shoes and got dancing again, until the next time. There would be and always was one of those. Joe shook his head, then finished his beer in a gulp.

"I hate that fucker, " he whispered as he caught sight of himself in the dusty mirror above the bar.

"I don't think he's so bad," a voice replied, eel slippery.

Joe turned and saw the small redhead two stools down. Took inventory of her bare legs, exposed shoulders, and large breasts. Her narrow nose and thin lips. Her deep eyes and the way she held her head, slightly tilted like the best pet. Joe wished he had more beer. He smiled as he moved down to the empty stool beside her.

"And what might your name be?" He leaned in close, a little too.

— 11 —

Notebook #31, page 23, only words on page:

Love can be both sweet water and vinegar, from teat to final sip. It can coat parched lips like fine sugar or crushed glass, and we will lick it away with eager tongues. The soothing liquid, suddenly salty and threaded red as it coats our throats but leaves us dying of thirst, which is just how we like it.

— 12 —

Eyeing up the middle of June

Marlin had been in love with Lisa Waller since she was Lisa Lloyd and had sat behind him in eighth grade social studies.

What began with notes passed over shoulders about how dull the class was and what kind of music was good, turned to mildly flirtatious taunts and invitations to things neither one of them were brazen enough to consider seriously. Between junior and senior year, Lisa had taken a boyfriend and that fact had torn a wound in Marlin's scarred-since-birth heart. He stayed close to her, smiled as directed and longed inside for a chance to make her his own. But even when the door of opportunity was left slightly ajar, hungry for his foot to keep it from closing, he'd sit still and watch it slowly shut.

The closest to telling Lisa how he felt was the day he admitted he had never kissed a girl and she had stopped by the trailer while his mama had been at work and showed him how it worked. Simple as that. Just one. Then, she scooted out the back door and hopped in her car and was gone. To her and those around them, it was a thing that never was. To Marlin, that kiss was a jewel in the safe of his soul. He still felt it whenever he saw her around town. Perhaps a feeble wave or nod but mostly, a cage of scurrying things is what his chest would become when their paths would cross…as though all the years were just trees blurring by on an afternoon drive.

Then, she called and asked him to meet her for lunch.

Then, she stopped by the garage one morning just to say hello. He stared at the floor while he returned her greeting. His insides were as Charybdis, always biting, churning, and swirling, and Lisa's return to his life did nothing to quell that feeling.

"What're you thinking about?"

Lisa's voice was the buzzing of bees. Each word, the whisper of light wind through lilac; beautiful and terrifying all at once. He held the steering wheel tighter than necessary, given that the truck was parked and the engine off. If he closed his eyes, he could hear himself turning to paper, begging to be crumpled up and thrown away or maybe burned like the best bridges. He looked over to where she sat and smiled. Her blue eyes were alien creatures. They knew stars and depthless black and he was jealous. He wanted to know them, too. Her lips curled into a smile as she repeated her question. He noticed the right side of her mouth was red-making-introductions-to-purple, the flesh raised.

"Minnows." Marlin spoke softly, a timid tongue-tying faulty knots.

"What?" Her brow furrowed as she sifted the word.

"My thoughts, they're always like minnows. Dozens of them. All of them small, but swimming fast. gasping when I catch 'em." He smiled and she caught it, badly mirrored it.

"I don't think that's true. You never could think small, Marlin Stains."

In one deft move, her slender hand was resting on his, like a ghost that suddenly appeared in a dark hallway. It wasn't there and then it was. Soft and scary as hell. Marlin's heart raced, his mind jabbered, and he felt as if he was burning alive. It was the best feeling he'd ever felt.

Until she spoke again and shot it dead.

"Marlin, I need to ask you a question, maybe a favor…"

She leaned close and looked him right in his blue eyes. He tossed his gaze at the dashboard, never one to go steady with eye contact. Her hand never left his, in fact, it squeezed harder, and her thumb rubbed the small scar on the web of his. His brain seized that second to remind him of how he got that scar when he stuck his hand down a gopher hole when he was four and the occupant was none too happy with the intrusion and bit him. That jump-cut to a memory of his father pulling the small rodent from his hand and throwing it against the stone steps, the small red smudge on the rock that stubbornly stayed for the rest of the summer, then taking the boy into the house to clean his wound.

Marlin refocused and saw Lisa's expectant eyes. He felt tears threatening as was often his go to when overwhelmed emotionally. He looked at her, then out the back window at Mr. Scott's field where a man on a tractor was drawing deep lines in the soil, his old beagle trotting along behind at a safe distance.

"What is it?" He managed. The question coming out like a desiccated thing.

"Do you remember when we were kids…when we were younger? Not little, but still young enough for innocence or maybe I mean ignorance."

"There isn't much difference between the two." Marlin mumbled.

Is there an age limit for ignorance?

"I was dating that boy and you liked me but were too shy

to do anything about it." Her eyes twinkled as she spoke. Star shine that he had never stopped basking in for all these years. "I knew it and I liked you too. My daddy didn't think too highly of you and so I had to keep seeing Jamison but inside I liked you. So much. You were so quiet and strange." Her voice evaporated and she studied Marlin. She touched his chin, turned his face to hers. Marlin smiled wanly and nodded.

How could I not remember all of that? I've never stopped feeling like that. Have carried it all these years.

"I'm still Quiet and Strange. In all capital letters." Marlin chuckled dryly.

"You've not changed but I have, this wilted wicked world sure has." A cloud passed over the sky of her face, the bit visible from the drapery of her hair, and darkened it.

"Joe has. Sometimes I feel like one of the lightning bugs we'd catch as kids and keep in a jar. I remember being awed and excited by their shine and glow and then devastated a few days later when they were just dead bugs in the bottom of a jar. That's how I feel anymore, Marlin. I'm one of the fireflies in the jar and Joe is the mean kid that caught me, he has his sweaty thumb over the air holes and I'm trying my damnedest to light but all I'm doing is drowning dry."

Marlin licked his lips; he coughed lightly before speaking.

"What are we driving to here?" It came out more abruptly than intended.

"Marlin…what would you do if someone hurt me?"

Her words hung in the air between them as Marlin's mind tore down and rebuilt a hundred scenarios at once. His brows met in the middle of his face, an arrow pointing down to a crooked nose. He looked her in the eyes and held fast.

"Why? What's he done?"

Lisa pulled her long hair back, the bangs and curling pieces that framed her pretty face and let him see.

— 13 —

Smack Dab in the Middle of June

"Hey, Marlin, you hear some sonofabitch robbed Goecker's store?"

"I hadn't. Goecker's? They sure didn't get away with a fortune." Marlin stared at his shoes, scrutinized the oil stains on the worn-through steel toes.

"Dint take no money at all. Stole all the fuckin' mirrors though. All the ones in the housewares aisle and the ones from the changing room doors and them big round ones in the ceiling corners to catch shoplifters, the ones from the bathrooms. Hell, they even pried the mirrors off the delivery truck behind the store!"

"Bizarre. What is that about?"

"No idea. Kinda weird. But then, when ain't shit weird around here? Maybe it was a vampire?"

"Um. No, Vampires don't cast any reflection so why would they steal mirrors?"

"It was a joke."

"Oh. Well, not a very good one," Marlin nodded and chewed on his bottom lip a second before addressing his boss once more.

"Sorrel…Can I ask you something?"

"Sure, and you sweet pea, for the millionth time, can call me Sore. Fire away!"

"I got kind of a problem."

"No such thing as kind of a problem. There is just no problem and problem, with problem coming in a variety of shapes, colors and sizes." Sorrel smiled so wide it showed that black eye tooth he had.

Marlin sighed. "Okay, I have a problem."

"I'm not entirely sure how you've managed to stay among the livin' here on this good goddamned earth for as long as you have with that rusty can of rocks you got for a brain there."

For punctuation, Sorrel Mosser tapped his temple with a thick finger tipped with a grease-clogged fingernail. The older man sneered, and it cracked and allowed a full smile to blossom. This tumbled into raspy laughter that soon had him smacking his knee for emphasis.

Marlin stared at Mosser's leg, just above the knee, where his prosthetic had gapped enough to show the line of crusted dirt and dried sweat that banded across the pale skin. His grip on the screwdriver in his hand tightened.

Mosser calmed himself and leveled a look at the younger man. The lack of smile on the boy's face was a stony wall in the open space of the garage.

"Boy, you know I'm funnin' ya. I mean, you do get yourself in some shit, but I like ya. Hell, I wouldn't keep you on here if I didn't."

Mosser picked at something between his top teeth with one of those offensive fingernails, examined what he extracted and wiped it onto his pale tongue. The jovial nature that had been present bled out like a stuck hog hanging. Mosser pulled the switch box from where it hung and thumbed a button. There was a mechanical groan as the bay door rolled down and separated the two men from the comfort of daylight.

"So, tell me what you've gotten tangled in this time." Mosser's voice was rawhide thick and just as rough. He opened the old Sucrets tin in his hands and removed a sloppily rolled cigarette. It looked like a mummified finger. He sat it on his lip and struck a match to seal its fate.

"Gimme the poop?" Mosser asked again, winking as the smoke rolled up into his lazy eye.

Slowly, Marlin started talking.

— 14 —

Mosser just stared at him. The right corner of his mouth almost raised in a half-assed grin. The room was fogged with acrid smoke from his cigarettes. Marlin sat still and stared at the floor, his brain creating faces and pictures in the oil stains on the concrete. There was a name for it, seeing faces everywhere, but he couldn't remember what it was. His mama called it *a poor man's Rorschach test*. Mosser stood and moved to the small refrigerator beside the workbench. It had once been white, but years of oily hands and greasy fingers had erased that.

Mosser grabbed a brown bottle from inside and popped the cap off against the edge of the door. He said nothing before he gulped the bitter beer down. He dropped the empty bottle into the crate at his feet before he turned to Marlin. He buttoned on a smile before speaking.

"You really got yourself in what we call a pickle. A sour-ass-dipped-in-donkey-piss-pickle, at that." Mosser took the last cigarette from his tin and lit it, then sucked a deep lungful of smoke, shaking his head as he did so.

"I am well aware. I don't really know…" Marlin mumbled. If Mosser heard him, he gave no acknowledgement.

"Men like Joe, they're like the Hydra. You know what that is, son?"

Marlin cringed. This meant Mosser was in one of his haughty intellectual moods and that he'd have to endure some ramble. Folks had been known to fossilize during the time it took Mosser to get to the fucking point when he was feeling all Professor smarty-pants.

He looked into the man's eyes and muttered his response: "A giant snake."

"Well, I guess that's correct but the Hydra was a snake with nine heads. It had one real head that if removed would kill the beast, but the other heads…if lopped off would cause two more to grow in its place. This problem you've gotten yourself mired in… that's what we call a Hydra dilemma. There is one solution, but it's nestled down among many outcomes that bite you in the ass and will blowback." Mosser sucked the life from his cigarette, dropped it on the floor, and crushed it under heel.

"I know what I ought to do." Marlin tried to sound assertive and even used his Adult-Even voice.

"Ought to and should do don't often match, Son. Ought is very rarely should and should is nearly never will." Mosser's eyes seemed wild, much whiter visible than usual. He was in a higher gear, for sure.

"I just don't know."

From outside the garage door came the blast of a car horn. Mosser winced and looked at the younger man across the room. "That's that asshole Seiders, he's here to get that piece of shit Corolla inspected. Sit tight and don't make no plans or do nothing yet. There're facets here you ain't aware of…I'm not at liberty to divulge 'em but it does offer me a unique perspective on your problem. Lemme have a think, I'll see if I can come up with a solution, maybe one that doesn't involve no injury, death or jail time."

Marlin said nothing, just nodded. Mosser was thumbing the button box, the door was going up and by the time Seiders had pulled into the garage, Mosser was sitting there alone, smiling like a kid on Christmas morning.

— 15 —

Notebook #45, Page 33, only words on page:
Sing with me, boys & girls:

Ain't no quiet like that cancer quiet. For a thing that devours so, that eats with endless appetite. An existence of gnaws and swallows, so complete. A hungry God (aren't they all?) that eats to remake in its own vile image. Its teeth are silent and the chewing invisible to the ear, It reduces the healthy to rag and bone, then comes back to the head of the line with an empty plate in skeletal hands.

"Please, Sir, I want some more…"

— 16 —

That Night

His mother was sleeping in the recliner again, the old yellow tom cat by her side, snoring in feline harmony. The low sigh of her breathing was amplified by the mask over her mouth, tethered by tubing to the green cylinder that stood behind the end table. The television was turned so low it was practically muted, but he'd seen every episode of *M*A*S*H* so many times he needed no sound. He was about to go out to the kitchen for some coffee when he heard him.

"Hey baby brother."

Marlin frowned, not because it was weird talking to his dead brother, the brother he had choked out in utero, but because said brother held a delusion that he was somehow older. Marlin looked down and saw the gray cat. It had a baby's face, kewpie doll round and smiling. Blue eyes that twinkled. It had stopped unsettling him years ago.

"Hi, Merle. Decided to brave a visit at Mama's tonight?"

"She sees me all the time, but I'm just a regular cat for her. For you, oh lucky brother of mine, I take my mask off."

"Ain't you considerate." Marlin poured a splash of milk into his mug and reached for the cap, before manners took hold, "You want some milk?"

"Sure." The cat smoothed against his legs, and it made every hair on Marlin's neck stand at attention. He sat the old butter dish on the floor and the cat began lapping at the contents, though the level in the dish never changed. Marlin sipped at the coffee and looked out the window. The wounded sun had limped off to die and the moon was standing in. The thermometer on the sill claimed it was a cool evening.

"I'm going out on the porch. I don't wanna wake her."

It was four long drinks of coffee before Merle joined him, jumping up on his brother's lap, only to be cuffed lightly across the back of the head. Marlin shook his head and frowned at the creature. "Never on me, dammit, how many times I got to tell you?"

"Sorry, force of habit." The cat smiled, cherubic cheeks rising to reveal rows of tiny points.

"What do you want?" Marlin sounded done.

"Sometimes, I think you don't like seeing me, little brother." Merle stopped and stood statue still as a mouse scurried across the end of the porch. The minute hovered in the warm mist that rose from the grass. "Sorry, I was distracted. So, what's new with you?"

"Oh, not much. Still stuck in this husk of a town, writing in my notebooks because I'm too afraid to send it anywhere or share it with anyone. Watching cancer eat our mother in ragged bites and oh, yeah, a girl I've had a crush on all my fucking life showed up to tell me her husband beats her, and I think she wants me to kill him and here I am drinking coffee and discussing it with my dead brother who appears to me in the form of a cat with a baby's face. So, yeah, everyday no-frills typical summer shit."

Marlin sat his mug down hard on the arm of the chair, the *thunk* bouncing off into the valley. The cat just sat there smiling. Quite Cheshire.

"Oh, brother, you do get in it. And I am very limited in what I can say in these exchanges. I mean, there are rules and etiquette that even I must adhere to. As to your writing, I have read-heard what you come up with and I think it's a damn crime you aren't sharing it. Write it down, send it off, I guarantee someone will like it and be happy to release it to the world. Some will love it, but just remember what the world does to things it holds dear…"

Marlin nodded and stared into the shadows where the truck was parked.

"I know watching Mama is hard on you. I saw you go through the same with Dad years ago. I can offer no solace other than her pain will be gone soon. She will be at peace."

"God, I hope so. Merle, is she going to heaven?"

The cat looked out into the yard, one of his icy blue eyes caught the reflection of the moon. "Sure," he answered a little too quickly.

Marlin held out his hand and the cat smoothed against his palm, the fur silky and soft, yet sent a current of odd electricity through him, making his insides dance. He looked down into that childish face and smiled a weak and sad smile. Something shifted in his gut.

"Guess it's my burden. Been doing time for murder my

whole life. You know I'm sorry, don't ya, Merle?"

"Of course, I do. You didn't strangle me; we were two babies sharing a saltwater shoebox with a mile of rope bunched between us. It was an accident. Besides, through you, I've seen what this world can offer and, frankly, I got the lucky end of the deal, you can keep it."

"So true."

"About the girl. I would suggest not killing the man. Maybe beat him up, maybe get her to go away with you or without, maybe stay the hell out of it…but I think murder is not a good look for you…for anyone, really."

"Probably, not. I do love her though. Have for half my life."

"I don't know if love is the fairest term, you've been smitten, I know. I've smelled it on you for a long time now. But love, that's a gamier stench and while I catch a whiff here and there, it ain't overpowering on you. That whatever you have for the girl, that might feel like forever, but guilt won't ever wash off your hands. Another man's blood will stain deep and dark. You can spell condemned either way."

Marlin nodded and looked down at his brother. The cat was staring at the sky, but his eyes seemed far away.

"You already know how this pans out, don't you?" Marlin sighed and leaned back in the chair, the wood groaning as he did so. The cat remained silent.

"You remember the first time we talked?" Marlin spoke again, looking up at the underside of the porch roof, at the snow of the soft spider webs nested there.

"Lemme see, I believe that would have been the church jamboree picnic that Mom dragged you to during one of her *Get right with the Lord* phases. You wandered off and sat in the cemetery and I showed up and told you I was your angel. You sat there talking to me so loud and long that Pastor Glunt thought your cheese musta slid off your cracker."

"And then I fed you that piece of ham I had been carrying in my pocket."

"I ate that shit, lint and all, not even sure why…I'm not even corporeal."

"Well, it was weird, but I've had a lot of years to get used to it, and I like having you around. I often wonder what it'd been like to play with you and run the fields and grow old with you at my side like real brothers."

"It'd be just like it was supposed to be. My absence would have come about another way. And with love and time invested, it would have been much more difficult. A house built by your own hands and sweat is harder to burn down."

The cat put a paw on Marlin's leg and stared up at him.

"Little brother, may I sit on your lap? I feel you need it and maybe me a little too…"

Marlin didn't look down or speak, but lifted his folded hands from his lap, affording enough space for the cat to hop up and curl itself into a small circle of gray fur.

Merle laid his head on Marlin's hand and whispered, "I love you, brother, and no matter what I'll be by your side."

Marlin began to snore soon after, and a while after that, the night sky flickered with bright, and a soft rain began to fall.

— 17 —

Joe sat at the counter of the kitchen island and ate the last spoonful of his Cream of Wheat. He stared at the television on the wall in the living room and tried to make out what he was watching without sound. The man in the suit with the severe look on his face and the ticker running across the bottom let Joe know he probably didn't care anyway. He finished his breakfast and got ready for work, buttoning his stained jeans, and stepping into his boots. Thing about being the garbage man was you didn't have to put on airs.

He was about to tie them when the phone rang. There was always a second of nostalgia when it happened, as most folks no longer had a landline, let alone an old ringer style of phone. He grabbed the receiver and held it to his ear.

"Yeah?"

"This Joe?"

"Yeah, who is this? "

"An old friend."

"Ain't got none of those, old or new. Who the fuck is this?"

"How's Lisa? Her bruises healin'?"

Joe stared at the phone as though through some perverse power, it had, in fact, turned to shit at his touch. His brows met as his brain tried to work out where he recognized this voice from. It seemed familiar.

"I heard you slammed her pretty good." The voice on the other end kept talking.

"I don't know what you are on about?"

"Don't play dumb. I know you hit her and have been, probably still are. Ain't no such thing as a secret in a small town. I know other things as well."

"The fuck does that even mean?" Joe was growling, his nerves hollering through gritted teeth for a blast of nicotine.

"It means, you sloppy caveman, that you slapped her for the first time or the thirteenth…that she told someone and that someone might aim to get even with you for it. For her. I mean, I wouldn't blame 'em…Lisa is a fine, fine piece of ass. And any man who hits a woman is garbage as we all know…a Garbage man." The caller chuckled over the line, and it was full of rust.

"You watch too much TV, Sunshine. My wife is my business. I have no idea what you're on about or up to, but you stay away from me and her. I know your voice, I ain't placed it yet but I will…" Joe paused, as if thinking were heavy lifting and his spine was about to crack under the weight.

"She told someone, and someone told another, ears abound in a small town." The voice on the other end admonished.

"*If* anything like that *had* happened and *if* she told anyone, it was probably that weirdo pal of hers who don't do nothing but spend time in his head or watching his mother dry up. Shit, the day I'm scared of that spooky faggot is the day I shoot lasers out of my eyes and dick. Now, who the fuck is this?"

"A friend, as I stated."

"Listen, *Friend*, trying to blackmail a man in a shit town for smacking his wife seems like an exercise in futility. I doubt I'm the only one."

"Right, but…Joe…if it were reported and it brought authorities to sniff around your door, what other odors might they pick up on? Maybe the stench of what you got growing out in field B behind the wall of dead school buses? Perhaps whatever it is stinking in the blue drums buried under the back part of the lower lot, right next to the little league field? I heard that company thickened your wallet good for that deal."

"I will find out who you are, and I swear on all that is Holy…"

"You seem awful mad for an innocent man. Just think about this position and I'll get back to you *very* soon." The caller spoke and then there was a click when he hung up, but Joe sat for a long moment in disbelief. His pores oozed sweat, yet he found himself shivering. His ribs hurt from the anger that was welling up inside of him. Joe was red-faced by the time he actually hung up the phone. He looked out the window and saw Lisa's car wasn't in the driveway.

Sometimes there is such a thing as luck and it smiles on you, gossip girl, he thought as he tied his boots and stomped to the door.

Across town, Mosser sat in his closed garage, hand still on the phone, his laughter spreading dark wings until it turned to coughing. Until he could barely breathe. Him thinking that this was entirely too much fun to be having before nine o'clock in the morning.

— 18 —

"You need to eat somethin', Ma."

Marlin leaned forward from the edge of the sofa and held the bowl of broth out to the woman in the recliner.

"Honey, I don't even have it in me to hold the bowl. I'm that weak today. Every day, and don't get me started about this damn air hose." She struggled to sit up a little as Marlin pushed another pillow down behind her. She fell back and closed her eyes, breaths coming faster and fogging the mask.

"I can swap the mask for the nose plugs thing so you can eat. And I'll hold it. I'll even spoon it to ya, but you need to eat a little."

The woman tried again to hoist herself up into a higher seated position, the bones in her back crackling like twigs underfoot. She made a pained face but finished the work, and once upright, made a point to button on a big fake smile for her boy. Marlin returned it with one of his own. The bowl of stock had cooled but was warm enough. He fed his mother in the dim light of the television. She managed four spoonful's of broth before allowing herself to slouch back down into her pillows and blankets. Within what seemed like seconds, she was snoring.

Around the foot of the recliner, slunk the gray cat with a baby's face and the saddest eyes.

"Howdy little brother."

Marlin just stared at it and wiped the tears that leaked from his eyes. He sat the bowl on the end table, sat still and quiet for a moment. Merle pawed his way into the kitchen and sat by the stove until Marlin got up and followed.

"She's fading." He managed, his breath hitching.

"She is, brother, she is."

"Fading fast."

"Fast is for bandage pulling and slow is for glaciers. Sorrow and grief is a bit of both."

"I don't have any more room for holes, Merle."

"What the hell does that even mean?" The cat spoke, little lips moving, whispery words floating from it.

"I feel like a core in a world full of shiny apples. I seem to be made up wholly of absence. My childhood was halved because you were gone. Then I got a Dad-shaped hole in my heart and now I'm making another space for another loss... digging another hole. I grew around those voids like a paper hornet's nest. I'm always empty but so full of buzzing..." Marlin shook his head.

A few tears dropped to the floor, and Merle licked them up before speaking.

"That's normal. What we lose makes up the most of us. Minus is usually equals. It's shadow worship of a sort."

Next to the last weekend of June

"Morning, Honey bun." Mosser stood back by the work bench. His plastic leg lay on the pitted wood surface before him, while his less-than-appealing stump rested on the stool next to his good leg. It looked like someone had sewn a dirty old softball where his knee should have been. He had a pair of pliers in his right hand.

"Morning, Boss. What are you up to?" Marlin picked a sleep booger out of the corner of his eye and wiped his finger on his pants.

"Went out drinkin' with Wade last night, and this damned leg has a piece of rough plastic or wire or something that's pissing ol' Stumper here the fuck off, so I'm trying to remedy the situation." He put the pliers down and went to filing the lip of the prosthetic limb with a piece of sandpaper.

The room started to smell like hot plastic and old sweat. It made Marlin wince.

"Smells kinda like Fritos, don't it? Them ranch ones." Mosser said and laughed at himself.

Marlin grimaced and swallowed hard.

Mosser dropped the grit paper to the bench and picked up his leg, blew the fetid dust from it, and balanced unsteadily as he pulled it back up onto the stump. He pushed the stool and watched it roll across the bay and rest against the taller tool chest. He then walked, slowly, to where it stopped and eased his bulk down. "That's much better."

"What's the cop car doing down at Enterline's? The masonry has been closed since he went upstate to tend to his mother."

"Vandals."

"Vandals? This place is turning into the mean streets of

New York as of late."

"Someone pried out all the mirrors from his trucks, somethin' like a dozen total as he got six of 'em."

"Again with the mirrors. That is bonkers."

"It certainly is. I heard old lady Canon chirping at the store that someone's been taking the mirrors from all the junked cars sitting around town. This is a redneck paradise, that has at least another two dozen vanity windows…"

"What did you say? Vanity what?"

"My grandpa called them that. Mirrors ain't nothin' but vanity winders, he'd say. I know what I look like, I don't need remindin'," Mosser said as he pulled his old cough drop tin from his flannel pocket and took out a smoke. He winked through the smoke at his employee and smiled. "So, you made any decisions yet?"

"No. I'm leaning heavily towards just trying to talk to him. But I worry that'll just buy her another beating. I can't call the cops…. we don't have none in this horse fart of a town. I thought I might take my hammer with me when I see him, just in case."

"Just in case is a fuse, boy. You take that tack and you'll be using that hammer. No spontaneity as you've already steeled yourself for a worse outcome."

"I don't know. I'm not good with confrontation. I could call him."

"You could do that." Mosser turned his head so the other man wouldn't register his smile. "A call is as good as a visit in the modern world."

"I just don't know yet."

"Thing is, whether you know it or not, the decision has already been made. The bones have been rolled and the pieces are being slid into their positions. Gotta remember, you ain't the only piece, not ever. By the time you decide to make your move, the game will be plotted out and you'll just be a piece moving on the board." Mosser lit another smoke from his tin, his fourth, and the room looked like the foggy crypt of an old Hammer film.

Marlin, who should have felt like Peter Cushing as Van Helsing, more accurately felt like the heart of Christopher Lee awaiting the kiss of the wooden stake.

— 20 —

Notebook #90, page 67, red pen:
"Acrimony is the devil's tongue, licking behind your ear before each whisper. Those whispers that flit about your mind like moths or ghosts. That nest in your heart like wasps or wanting. That squirm into your guts like tumor and boil.

You'll miss it when it isn't there…"

— 21 —

Mosser and his buddy, Wade Grubb, sat at the corner table of the bar, chain smoking beneath the *No Smoking* sign.

Mosser pushed the remaining bite of his pepper steak into that awful mouth of his, washed it down with the dregs of his beer. He burped loud enough to make heads turn and smiled and made a show of taking a bow. Wade giggled like a child.

"So, I made the first move yesterday. No, Tuesday. I called Joe and told him I knew what he was up to. He got hot, boy. I lit the fuse but good."

"So, what's the rub here? How's pissing off a wife beater pay off for us? I bet he ain't the only one to smack a bitch in this town." Wade ate a cold French fry, that blackened front tooth shining like wet slate.

"Well, I see it like this. He gets mad and it boils in him. Simmering is always good, deepens the flavors. He won't hit her because he knows people, or well, *someone* is watching. Or maybe he will, not the point here. We know some shit here, well, I do. We know some of his more, um, under the radar dealings. We know she ain't no saint. I went to school with her and while she ain't a slut or nothing, she has a way with the baton, so to speak." Wade's brow furrowed and Mosser sighed and shook his head.

"Not like them marching band girls with the flags and shit. Like a conductor of a symphony, pin dick. She knows how to play people and situations. Anyway, the second move is a follow up call with a request for some money. We threaten to divulge some of his dirty bruised secrets and ruin his business."

"Dude, he ain't the only cracker what hits his wife here… this ain't Matlock. Ain't gonna hurt his business, he runs the junkyard. Who cares who takes your trash?"

"Zip it. People put on airs. And this town is a sore that's dryin' up anyway, he can't afford to take even a little hit to the wallet…so he'll bite. Then, maybe we set up a meeting and get our money and shake hands and all is good."

"But he'll know us then and then he'll kick our asses every chance he gets. Or maybe clean his slate and call the cops."

"He ain't calling no cops and that's why god made masks, Sunshine." Mosser popped his old tin and withdrew the last home rolled it held. He lit it and made a dessert of the sour smoke and little bits of tobacco that peppered his tongue. Wade pushed his final fry around in the clot of gravy still on his plate, while Hank Snow sang to them from the jukebox in the corner.

— 22 —

"Marlin."

"Yeah." He coughed once, softly to try and dislodge the sleep sludge from his throat.

"It's Lisa."

"I know. What's up?"

"Just wanted to talk to you. Joe is acting really weird and I'm not at all sure what's brewing with him."

"He come at you?"

"Not at all, actually. He's being nice as pie and that's scarier than his knuckles." She managed a small laugh.

Marlin sighed heavily through his nose, which produced a slight whistle.

"What was that?"

"Mom's got the tea kettle on." The lie came easily.

"I'm not sure what to do. I feel like he knows I told you… or someone. It feels like a trap."

"Lisa. I can't do anything just yet. Bide your time, stay out of his way and be watchful. You sense danger, run like hell."

"You're going to help me escape?" Lisa sounded breathy.

"I am. I'm just not entirely sure how yet."

There was a click as she hung up the phone, and Marlin sat on the edge of his bed and looked at the receiver in his hand, like it was both a key and a lock.

— 23 —

On the other end of town, Lisa sat in the dark of her kitchen. Snores floated from the back bedroom down the hall where Joe slept. A smile crawled to her lips as she realized she could easily slink the length of their modular and cut his throat as he snored away, pull her foot from this snarl she was in and be gone. But where was the fun in that?

She pulled a cigarette from the pack of Winston's Joe had left on the table. She'd erase all traces of the smoke when she was done, like she always did. It was just another secret anyway. Secrets are like sweets, there's always room for one more.

— 24 —

Notebook #9, page 14, green pen (very faded):
"Let us not mistake chivalry for bravery. Hormones are the weakest of armor and the heart, the most uneven of stilts. Love is the lance that skewers the heart, often deepest when it is held and aimed by that same schizophrenic muscle."

— 25 —

July 3rd, almost Independence Day
Joe leaned against the counter of his office room at the scrap yard, which was in fact, the tail end of a small Toyota truck, cut off just before the rear axle and butted up to the wall on cinder blocks. It wasn't pretty but it was functional and yielded far more room than a typical desk. It held heaps of paperwork and small boxes of screws, washers, and lost bits from all manner of abandoned machinery. There were four ashtrays, one in each corner of the surface, and all were overflowing with ashes and butts. Empty beer bottles lined the back like soldiers. Pens and pencils and screwdrivers were strewn about like limbs on a battlefield. After he'd cut Leeny loose, he got rid of her desk, as looking at it made him mad and got him hard at the same time. It lived out by the pile

of washing machines, the surface he'd bent her over so many times now warped and cracked.

He stared out the large window, at the sprawling trash scape outside. Five square miles of dead cars, trucks, tractors, and boats. Mounds of moldering furniture and lumber. Pyramids of paint cans and pipes. He stared at it, and while that was where his legitimate income came from, it was the unseen refuse that paid for his house and the vehicles and kept his bank account portly. The taking on of waste materials from the cleaner factory, and the clinic outside of Burrville did.

Then, there was his sideline of providing a safely hidden grove for the local dope growers to nurture their crop, surrounded by a wall of derelict buses and campers and a stretched plastic tarp to hide from prying eyes in the sky. This was his empire. He built it from nothing, well, at least from the little salvage business his pap and uncles had begun back when Korea was still a police action and opinions weren't fences of razor wire.

He drummed his fingers and let the Winston in his mouth burn to the filter as his mind swirled and stuttered over things he'd done, decisions to be proud of, and some to be locked in the attic and shunned. He tried following them back to faces and names and figure out who might have called him. And just when he was about to call the mission, to crush the dead smoke in the ashtray and head out to do some actual work, that was when a face formed from the fertile mists in his mind. A face only a mother could love, and it would help if she were blind. Sorrel Mosser.

Sure! He'd worked here for years while saving up the dough for his own garage. Hell, half of the money he got came under the table and was from some of the more lucrative endeavors, and he knew about them. He knew and he'd never muttered

SNARL

a peep in all the years since…until now.

"Son of a bitch," was all Joe could manage before he stomped out into the falling drizzle and allowed the cool rain to soothe the fire in his blood.

— 26 —

Marlin kicked off his muddy boots just inside the door. He paused to listen for the soft voice of his mother and when it didn't greet him, hesitantly peered around the corner into the living room. She was in her recliner, her thin lids jumping in dream as little snores escaped her nose, her air tubes around her neck. Marlin frowned but felt relief at the rise and fall of her birdlike chest.

He set about heating a can of soup, and then sat in the porch rocker and watched the bats dive for mosquitos in the warm dim of late evening.

His brain was dancing, and he couldn't still it. He ate from the bowl and stared into the darkness, not trying to think about anything, hoping for a reset. He heard the slight skitter of pebbles and saw a blur of gray surge onto the porch.

"Hi, Merle," he said without really looking down at his brother.

"Hello, baby B. How are you getting along?"

"I'm here…"

The cat nodded, its large eyes reflecting the fresh moon.

"Mama is closer." Merle said with the calm tone that one might announce that vinegar was sour, or the sun was bright. Marlin could only nod.

The cat trotted closer and sat almost on his brother's socked feet, raised a paw, and pushed it against Marlin's calf. They remained still and quiet like that for a mile-long minute.

"You remember Mr. Wish?" Merle broke the cloud of quiet that enveloped them.

"I do. He was a crotchety old man, but he was nice…to me. He always kept an eye when I was outside."

"He was all of that and he did. He was fond of you. And he was made of secrets and glued together with guilt and regret. He struggled to wear the other suit every day. The one that occasionally smiled and offered a pleasantry."

"He did seem sad sometimes. A little bitter. Usually in the evenings when he drank and sat in the driveway."

"His days were arduous marathons. Did you know he went to war when he was fifteen? By the time he could legally drink, he had killed a dozen men…boys really, foreign but the same as him. And every one of them took a piece of him when their breathing stopped. The medals and the parades, they offer no real bandage to those kinds of wounds, Brother."

Marlin sat the bowl on the table, the spoon clanking loudly across the yard. He felt his eyes start to tear as he thought about his long dead neighbor and the burden he had quietly carried.

"You know his wife died while having their baby, a son that never knew breath?"

"I did not." Marlin licked his trembling lips. "Why are you telling me this? Some grand Scrooge parable lurking about?"

The cat allowed claws to appear and sank them into his brother's leg, just a little. Marlin pulled away and swatted at the cat who did not move.

"I just want you to realize that no one is just as you see. The person you see and know or think you do, has an entirely different person within themselves. Usually, a being of shadow and things that squirm from the brightness of light. Almost impossible to see a maggot in a pile of rice."

Marlin remained quiet and still. Down the street, someone yelled, and it was followed by a slamming door.

The cat lightly batted his brother's leg until he looked down once more, "I'm telling you that you will have a forever suit that will weigh as an anchor and hold you in place for secret miseries to pummel and pinch."

Marlin sighed and stood and as he opened the screen door, looked down at the cat and said, "Why couldn't you be like fucking Casper and just be all cheery and happy?"

"Because he's a comic book, Brother. This is real life."

Marlin chuckled as he went inside, and the cat was gone by the time the door creaked closed.

— 27 —

Mosser sat on a short stack of tires behind the garage. He squinted into the fresh sun as smoke from one of his cigarettes poked his eye. He knew Wade was coming around from the front of the building by the echo of his thick cough that reverberated off the brick walls. The dude needed to ease up on his smoking, and not just the cigarettes.

"Morning, Boss."

"Wade, I tell you often and again, I ain't your boss, you don't work for me. You work *with* me."

"It's just a saying. Like Sir or Buddy."

"I don't like that shit neither. I gotta name. My mother gave me a good one, so I'd prefer it used."

"Sorry, Sore. So where we at?"

"I called our boy again last night. He seemed really stirred up. I think we've poked the nest enough; we need to prepare to shit or get off the pot."

"What that means is?"

"It means I called him and told him what we demanded. How much. I didn't get greedy, I feel that 40K is a nice even number to half between us. We could even get out of this cow turd town if we wanted."

"An' he went with it?"

"He weren't happy but he didn't fuss, just called me a sonofabitch again and said it'd be waitin'."

Wade's mouth moved as he sussed out what his share of the amount would be and started to turn to a grin before Sorrel flicked it away.

"You ain't wastin' it on meth, boy."

Wade did not respond but sadly nodded and kicked at a bottle cap with his ragged sneaker.

"So tonight, after I close up, I call him gain and tell him when an' where to leave the money so we will pick it up all anonymous-like. We'll wear masks to be safe and we'll take one of the extra cars from the back lot that ain't gonna be recognized. It ought to go easy peasy."

"Then just like that we're done? No mess, just money?" Wade's question was heavy with hope.

"For now. That's the grand thing. We get through this unidentified and we can troop this trick out once in a while to fluff the financial pillows so to speak." Sorrel smiled big, his fetid teeth like jewels in a horror show crown.

Wade didn't return it. His worry lines deepened, and he pushed his hands further into his pockets, his already bony shoulders forming sharper points.

"Cheer up, Buttercup. It's gonna be fine. I ever steer you wrong before?" Sorrel used his fatherly voice. The deeper warmer tone that worked its fingers into Wade's tight muscles and jangled nerves.

"Not on purpose, no. This one has my stomach jumpy

for some reason." Wade stammered. He was trying to fish a smoke from his pack of Kools and work his lighter out of his jacket pocket at the same time.

"No?" Sorrel caught the tiny barb nested in his friend's response but ignored it. The kid was jumpy, he reeked of tweaking and Mosser didn't need that shit getting worse.

"Sure, the belly issue isn't on account of too much pot and crack and forgetting to eat?" Mosser dropped the butt of his home-rolled and plucked another from his tin.

Wade stared at him, trying to convey angry and mean but pulling off more of a scared and anxious look.

Mosser shifted gears. "Wade, go home and drink three cups of warm tea. No sugar, maybe a little honey. Set your alarm for seven tonight, set it loud. Then, get in bed and cover up, completely. Make a dark cocoon and wriggle down in it. You'll sleep well and good and when you get up, don't you *dare* smoke anything but Kools. You hear me, Boy?"

Wade remained silent and stared at the old Pennzoil sign that leaned against the wall. He was far off in his thoughts.

"Wade! You hear me?"

The younger man blinked and slowly nodded, "Yeah. I hear you."

"Get with it. I'll be by around five, give or take fifteen minutes, and we'll go over the plan again. I gotta go get the gun and clean it."

"Ok….wait, gun! You said nothing about guns, bro!"

"Dude, it's cool. It won't be loaded; I haven't had bullets for it for nearly fifteen years."

Wade looked unsure and terrified.

Mosser kept talking. "Also, be sure to wash your face. I got us some masks and they'll make you break out if you're all dirty and greasy under 'em."

"Thanks, Pop." Wade sneered as he walked back out of the alley.

Sorrel finished his smoke and taped together a plan to fit the mold of the lies he'd just told his accomplice.

— 28 —

July Seventh

"Where are you off to?" Joe's voice was calm, eerily so.

"Thought I'd hit the store, grab some stuff to make dinner. I was thinking maybe meatloaf."

Joe just gazed at her over the top of his glasses, the paper bent down like a gull wing. The more he stared, the more her cracks began to show. She held eye contact as well as a palsied man held a teaspoon of water. When she completely looked away, masking it as trying to find her wallet, he snapped the paper back to attention and spoke in a clear voice.

"Be back by dark. And don't be talking to anyone. There's too much gab in this town and people seem to know all kinda shit they oughtn't. Idle chatter is the devil's patter, my Nanny used to say."

— 29 —

Lisa held the wallet in her hand. She could tell he was still watching her squirm. She could feel his eyes gouging into her guts. Her spine danced and her cheeks flushed. When she was sure she could speak without her voice cracking, she replied. "I'm just getting what I need and coming home."

Joe said nothing, just kept pretending to read the news. She could have dragged it out. Gone whole hog with the "But I never talk to anyone" shit, but he knew, and she knew he did, and he knew *that*. This was part of the choreography she'd scored. She needed maybe one more push to get him to snap, and a call to her boy with fear in her voice and blood on her face and he'd come running to save her. And when the smoke cleared, she'd be free of Joe. She'd have his money and she'd slink off to another town and a start called Fresh. She jingled the keys and stomped to the door. "Be back directly." she said, and the door closed before Joe could grunt anything in response.

When he heard the car back out of the driveway, he allowed himself a smile.

— 30 —

Marlin stared at himself in the dirty pane above the sink. His gaunt cheeks were peppered with wiry beard growth. The bags beneath his blue eyes had bags of their own, the depth of his weariness ran that far.

He tried to remember when he had gotten to be like this, when he was a cabinet of many drawers and each of them holding secret spaces of their own, all of them brimming with loathing and worry of some sort. He was always quiet and not very social. In school, his infrequent outbursts were often ill-fated attempts at humor that ended up with him in the doghouse and another kid wanting to throttle him. He began writing to free the voice that ran rampant behind his eyes, the continual ribbon of dialogue that was in his voice yet not from his lips. He started filling notebooks and trying to fashion stories. Cohesive narratives were of the dodo bird to him, extinct oddities that others mentioned, yet he could not comprehend. He had sent out exactly eight stories in his lifetime and received responses for all of them, yet none had ever appeared in any print that was not his. He sighed and looked at his tired face once more, the reflection brazen now that the night was crawling in. He heard the recliner clunk into the sitting position, followed by the sharp gasp of his mother's faulty wheeze.

"Marlin, that you out there?" The words were phlegmy and thickly executed.

"I'm here, Mama. Just finishing up the dishes." He was hardly bothered by the ease of little lies these days. Hardly tasted them at all as they scampered from his mouth.

"Did you eat?"

"I did, Ma. I grabbed something when I stopped for gas. I was about to heat you some broth."

"Can you bring a piece of bread as well, to dip in it? I think I would welcome some texture."

"Sure." Marlin appeared in the doorway, moments later, a bowl in one hand, a paper plate with a piece of brown bread and a spoon in the other. He sat on the edge of the coffee table and gently brought a spoonful of broth to the woman's bluish lips. "Go ahead, it ain't too hot."

She sipped it and allowed the slight warmth to flow through her. Closed eyelids fluttered and she smiled. She had apparently been starving. He submerged a corner of the bread in the bowl and watched the brown deepen with the absorption. He moved it to her waiting mouth, and she took a bite. Her gray teeth easily chewing the soggy morsel.

"How are you, Son? You look so very tired."

"I'm ok. Just working a lot. Breaking my shifts up to be here with you more."

"I'm alright. You just work normally; I'll be here when you get home. Always have been."

Marlin smiled and nodded while something sharp gouged

him just under his tongue and tears filled his eyes. He hadn't deserved this woman.

"I'll consider it. Let's finish your dinner and get you a bath and ready for bed."

"I said before you ain't bathing me. That is not the natural order of things, a boy to have to wash his parents like they was babies. You help me into the bathroom, and I can manage."

"You gonna need me to take the extra tank in for you?"

"No, I can wheeze my way through a short bath. I'll be fine."

Marlin nodded. He'd learned decades earlier that arguing was futile, and he was in no mood to Quixote her stubborn windmills today. His brain was practically buzzing with activity. Grand Central Station teaming with fire ants.

While Mama was in the bathroom and he listened for any sounds of distress, he watched the nearly soundless news on the TV. Someone had stolen all the mirrors from that retro arcade in Steelwater, ZAP! The entire back wall of the place had been made of them. Marlin just shook his head and closed his eyes. He was snoring by the end of the commercial break.

— 31 —

Invoice Pad, Page 20, Black Ink:
To bear the weight of duty as well as that of longing and fate. Bouldering weights that tipple on the shoulders as I (we) walk our tightropes between expectation and extermination. Sour acrobats. Fearless fidgeters. Either way we end in a fall. Always. Accepted. Acclaimed.

— 32 —

Wade looked at Mosser and shook his head, shaking loose small flecks of dandruff onto the shoulders of his black Mötley Crüe t-shirt. Mosser held the other mask out to his friend, since he was obviously not too keen on the Popeye one.

"Fine, I'll be Popeye then. You be Casper. "

"Where the fuck did you land them masks, they're the old rubber-band-in-back kind from when we was kids. They don't even make that shit no more." Wade turned it over and looked at the back, the yellowish-brown staining around the nostrils and mouth. Something in his belly began to dance.

"My Nan never throwed anything away. When she died and I took over her house, that garage out back was a treasure trove. A goddamn time capsule. Over sixty years of all manner of bric-a-brac bullshit. They'll serve the purpose, Snootypants."

Wade pulled the smiling ghost's face over his and winced as the rubber band snagged his kinky long hair. That was exactly why he had hated them as a kid too. "Boo," he managed with absolutely no commitment at all.

"You are the worst, Wade." Mosser pulled the plastic visage of the sailor man down over his own. It made a marked improvement.

"What's the plan and schedule?" Wade practically whimpered; the words muffled.

Sorrel made a show of looking at his bare wrist, pretending there was a watch there.

"Go home and eat, shower, rub one out if you need to relax...then I'll be by for you around Seven. We'll head over to Joe's after I call and tell him to leave the money at the end of his walk. We barely stop, grab it, and get gone."

"Just like that, Sore? What about the gun?"

"Just to wave around if a scare is needed. Joe's all tough with knuckles and yellin' but I think he'd shy from a pistol. So yeah, just like that. Easy peasy. Real life is never as convoluted as the shit on television."

Wade pulled the mask off his face and frowned at the curled knot of his hair stuck where the rubber band was stapled to the edge of the plastic visage. He hated this whole idea, and his gut was telling him he was right to do so. His spine kept him right in line with it anyway.

"Okay," was all he managed to mumble.

— 33 —

Lisa walked down the aisle and stared at the canned peas, not actually seeing them. Her brain was fencing with itself. She had put the pieces on the board and had them lined up right, she thought, but now…

Now it just felt off, like she left the room and one of the players moved their piece slightly, but she could not actually recall the position so certainty was impossible. Joe was acting weird. Marlin weirder than usual. The overall atmosphere of it was just heavy.

She took a can of creamed corn and dropped it in her basket. She'd need to try and pay close attention until Marlin took Joe out of the picture and she was free again. God, she hoped Marlin was man enough to do it. She hefted another can from the shelf, lima beans, and as she added them to her order, daydreamed of going home, putting them in a sock and beating Joe's face into glorious mush.

Marlin sat in his truck. Merle was on the seat beside him. His whispery purring mingled with the country song at low volume, Loretta Lynn oozing from the door speaker.

"I ought just kill him. I mean, I can make it look accidental. Then Lisa would be safe, he'd be gone, and I can just take care of Mama until…"

"Until ain't far away at all, Baby B." The cat muttered. Marlin never took his eyes from the windshield and the world that was on the other side of it. From in here, it was always like watching television. Muted and not quite real.

"I don't know, I think I'm gonna go try and talk to him. I'll take the hammer. And I won't let it come to blows if I can help it."

His brother said nothing, just watched him as he talked. Old Missus Ford walked by and gave him a cursory look while pulling at the leash that connected her to her dog, probably wondering why he was sitting in a smoke-filled truck talking to himself so animatedly. Marlin stopped talking while he pulled the truck in gear but kept a boot firmly on the brake. He had to go home and check on Mama and then steel himself for a possibly heated confrontation. "I guess there's no time like the present," he exclaimed, looking over to see his passengers gone. The cigarette in the ashtray was crushed out and he had no recollection of doing it. The remaining smoke fading.

He pulled away from the curb. The old woman's dog barking and pulling at its leash as he drove into uncertainty.

— 35 —

Joe stood under the carport and watched the light drizzle water the lawn, the cooler air and dampness seemed to cause the fog from his cigarette to slither around him like a snake. He looked at the old suitcase on the floor. A small American Tourister job that was once bright teal, now, faded to a bilge water green, dulled by age and abuse. Inside, was maybe three hundred dollars in ones, rubber banded to stacks of cut newspaper, a few bills on top and a pair on the bottom so at quick glance the case seemed choked with cash. The deception had taken him the duration of an episode of *Bonanza* to put together.

"Good thing Sorrel is as dumb as he is ugly." Joe whispered to no one as he stomped the butt of his smoke under a dirty boot and opened his Jeep. He leaned across the seat and opened the glove box to remove the pistol that lived there. He looked at it and knew that Mosser would most likely show up armed, but he also knew the man hated guns and it would no doubt be for show only, so he put the gun back and locked the vehicle. His eyes fell to the corner by the edge of the porch and the assortment of tools that leaned there. Joe smiled as he walked over and grabbed the handle of the bush axe. The heft of it in his hands made him warm inside. The curved hook of its blade was twice as long as that of the regular one, more intimidating.

— 36 —

"I have to work a little late tonight, Mama. Sorrel asked me to clean up the shop and close for him, he had something going on." Marlin talked while he stared at himself in the bathroom mirror, the door open enough for him to see into the living room and make sure she was there and breathing.

"Ok, I'm very tired. I'm just gonna sleep until you get back. Pain is bad today, so much so I actually ate one of them pills that nurse fella left me."

The television reflected in the glasses on her nose, glasses that seemed so surreally large on her small thin face. He nodded and spit into the sink, rinsed the mouthwash spittle down the drain. He thought he caught a glimpse of gray fur from the corner of his eye, but when he turned, there was nothing.

"I won't be real late, Ma. Ought to get home by nine-thirty. I can bring some pizza if you'd be up for it? The sausage and onions kind you like."

"No thanks, Honey. My stomach feels like anything is just a torpedo borin' through anymore. Just some saltines might be nice. Soak up the acid."

Marlin took packet from the box of crackers from the top of the fridge, opened and sat them on the arm of the recliner. He looked at the woman who made him and how much like an effigy she seemed these days.

"I can move you to the bed, Ma. I'll angle the TV so's you can still see your shows."

"I'm fine here, Marlin. I can make the three steps to the bed if I need ta. Go do your job and I'll see you later." She craned her head up for him to kiss her forehead, which he did. The greasy sweat that touched his lips tasted bitter.

What did you expect death to taste like, boy?

The voice in his head belonged to Mr. Wish. Always quick to cut through it, he was. Marlin tied his boots and slipped out the door and into the waning after-rain sunshine.

— 37 —

Marlin looked at the pile of trash he'd just swept up, and decided Sorrel was a pig. There were easily a hundred cigarette butts and easily twice as many bottle caps, it seemed. Incorporated with the bits of glass, metal shavings, bolts and nuts and plastic wire bark and other scraps of typical garage offal, the pile was as big as a large groundhog. He pushed it into the dustpan and dumped it in the box that would go in the burn barrel out back on the next dry day. He sat down in Sorrel's chair and leaned back, closed his eyes, and thought about his less than cunning plan.

Go to Lisa's and knock. When Joe answers, just tell him you're on to him and to stop hitting her or you're going to have to stop him, and you aren't afraid to involve the authorities.

That time the voice was that of his mother, dripping with worry and uncertainty, while trying to be practically stern. He sat forward and the springs in the seat groaned. He walked over to the tool bench and hefted the hammers, seeing if he could maybe upgrade from the small home model he had in the truck. These were about the same, so he left them. His would have to do. The Dr. Pepper clock above the oil drum had the time as going on seven. It'd be dark soon. He flicked off the lights and let the shadows fondle him for a few minutes before he moved.

— 38 —

Lisa slid the last plate into the sink and watched it disappear beneath the soapy water, wishing she could pull a vanishing act that easily. She dropped the fork in her hand, and it landed on the bottom with a muted *thunk.* She turned to retrieve the remaining glasses from the table and found Joe immediately behind her, looming large. "Joe! You gave me a start."

The smirk that squiggled his face was a thick wormy thing. His eyes remained icy stones. "I was actually thinking about givin' you a finish. That mouth of yours." He pushed her, not hard enough to topple, but enough to make her flail a little. She felt the edge of the sink counter gouge her backbone.

"Joe, I'm sorry. For whatever. Whatever it was this time. The meat was a little more done than you like but…" Her voice was timid and trembling, inside she was nodding at herself.

This is it, girl, this is the pin pulled…

"I love you, Lisa. But man, I gotta say there are times when you work your fingernails under the scab and give it a hard yank and then I wanna pound you. You always knew how to make that madman dance. Shit, when we was first married, I never knew there was a madman until you started to coax him out." He stopped and she backed up sideways along the counter, small steps toward the back door.

"Yeah, I cheated…a time or two. Maybe three if a hand job counts. But I always provided. I paid the bills. Kept you in clover and got our girl away at school…all paid for. And all I asked for was a little respect. Decorum, is that a word…shit, it is, I heard it before but I'm not sure what it means, but I'm leaving it here."

The open hand met her cheek before she realized she'd rolled her eyes.

"Yeah, I know, little Miss Smart Bitch. That word probably don't mean what I used it for, but I don't much give a fuck. That mouth of yours. That goofy weirdo boyfriend of yours. I have some people coming for money to keep them from going to the cops about me. About *my* business. All because that mouth of yours that you can't keep closed."

Lisa held a shaking hand against the fire blossoming on her face. She swallowed and felt her lips trying to curl into a smile. She bit her tongue and looked up into Joe's dull eyes.

"Joe, I never said anything to Marlin. We're just friends. You know that. I hid the bruise when I met him for lunch a while back. I swear. I don't know what you're talking about." She took another step, only three more from the door.

Another, now only two.

Joe's size eleven boot swept into her calf, and she went down, the back of her head connecting with the counter as she did. She came to rest and remained still, a thin trickle of blood running down her slender neck. Joe began to kneel over her when he heard the rumble of an engine out front.

"Hold please," he sneered before he stood and stormed into the living room and through the front door, pausing only to grab the axe that leaned beside the front door.

— 39 —

Wade hadn't even fully braked when Sorrel had his door open and was jumping out of the old Dodge. He hunched over and sort of jogged to the end of the front walk where a suitcase sat below the mailbox. His breathing quickened beneath the mask, and he turned briefly to give his partner a thumbs up. The bang of the door and the big man stomping his way made him stop cold.

"I fucking *knew* it was you, you fat sonofabitch!" Joe's strides were eating up distance like hungry rats. Sorrel put up his empty hand and started to panic.

"Now, Joe. This was only…um…a joke, you know. A gag…I don't much care if you wanna smack that bitch around." He did his best to retreat, not at all in a graceful way thanks to his old-school prosthetic. He saw Joe slow and raise the arm he had hidden behind his back, watched the arm extend to a thick wooden handle that ended in a shining curved blade.

"Joe, on all that is holy, we was gonna bring the money back in a day or so. Have a big ol' laugh about it. Honest. "

"Shut that fucking stink hole mouth. The only thing worse than the breath leaking out of it, is the lies." Joe swung the handle and the wood connected hard with the fat man's arm. The suitcase hit the ground and popped open, exposing the bundles of money. Sorrel almost forgot the excruciating burning of his freshly broken elbow at the sight of it. He looked back to Joe in time to see him raise the axe again, back over his shoulder like he was preparing to win the summer beer and baseball classic at the pavilion. Sorrel shook his head, the words flowing from his mouth were terrified babble.

"Stop right fucking there!"

Joe stopped mid swing and Sorrel turned in the direction of the shout, still feeling the urine that soaked him, that was seeping into his plastic leg. Wade strode past the fallen man and right up to Joe Waller, fists at his side until he planted himself in front of his fallen friend. Without so much as a word, the kid swung his right arm around and Joe had a literal second to register the large screwdriver in it before the length of the business end disappeared between his ribs. Wade stepped back and turned to help Sorrel up and paused only when he saw his friend frantically shaking his head. Wade turned in time to see Joe's sneer and his shoulders follow through just before his vision swam upward and he saw only dim night sky and faded as he saw the car at the end of the driveway, upside

SNARL

down. After Joe swung the second time Wade's head fell into Mosser's piss-soaked lap.

Sorrel Mosser had not screamed since he failed to outrun the train when he was fifteen, but he was screaming now.

— 40 —

Napkin, found in Notebook #45. Black ink:
The fuse of fate is easily lit, by finger, by match, by deed or by tongue. The fuse fizzles and sputters and burps to the flames of destiny, where only the water of tears is liable to extinguish the hungry fire.

— 41 —

Marlin offed the headlights and slowed as he made the turn onto Lisa's street. He saw an old green Charger idling at the end of the driveway and had turned off his own engine before his brain had successfully deciphered the panoramic nightmare that was being carried out before him.

He felt his muscles stiffen as he watched. Two men in masks were standing in the drive, facing Joe.

Joe had an axe and had just hit the fatter masked man in the arm with it. Even from his distance he heard the crack of snapping bone. The bigger man went down, and the other masked fella moved forward and punched Joe in the chest, Marlin could see a dark bloom on Joe's pail denim shirt. Joe swung the axe and the masked man's...

Is that a Casper mask?

...head left his shoulders, falling into the other man's crotch where he sprawled on the concrete. Then the scream, rising like a rocket into the fresh night sky.

Marlin went stone still and found that he had nearly stopped breathing. His hand grabbed for the door handle but could not himself to open it and get out. "My God," he whispered in what could almost be a mantra. He pushed it open enough to allow the full volume of the screams to greet him. He knew without a doubt that it was Mosser and that meant the beheaded man could only have been Wade. He slid out and knelt along the driver's side bumper of his truck. Low and out of sight, he watched. The hammer he had fretted about lay on the passenger side seat.

— 42 —

"Jesus fuckin' Christ, Joe. You killed Wade! You fucking killed Wade!"

Joe snarled, and it was bestial. He swung the axe in a lowly sweep, blade backwards so the brunt of the metal butt connected with the cowering man's knee. There was a hollow *thunk* and then Mosser's lower leg was off and sliding a few feet away.

Mosser dropped his friend's head and awkwardly crab-walked, crookedly with one leg, but made some strides towards the car running in the street. He saw the shadow that devoured the slight bit of light that guided him and turned in time to see Joe swing at him. He screamed as he assumed the blade was about to separate his head from his shoulders but was only dazed by the heavy crack of the club across his nose. He felt warm thick blood pour from it. The salty droplets that hit his open mouth were his own piss that had drained down into the leg moments earlier. Mosser looked back to see Joe taking a batter's stance again, in his grip the ankle of his own goddamn prosthetic leg, He almost smiled despite himself, but that was the second Joe swung for the fences, The hard plastic decimating the remains of Mosser's nose and the swelling flesh of his cheeks splitting open to bleed themselves.

"Pleashe. Mah Gahd Pleashe!" The words tripped over the loose teeth that dangling in the wreck of his mouth.

Mosser dropped flat, face up to the fresh moon as blood gushed from his face. Joe stepped over him and raised the leg once more.

"Pleash, Joe. I begguh yuh, Pleash." One of the teeth found freedom and fell onto Mosser's chest where it shined like a pearl.

Joe brought the limb down. Raised it. Brought it down. Raised it and brought it down. He only ceased when Mosser's head was just a flat thing oozing gray and red on his driveway. He dropped the leg to the ground, the moon shining off the dark blood dripping from the aged plastic.

— 43 —

Marlin knelt with his forehead against the cool metal of the bumper, his heart racing and his hands shaking, what he had just witnessed was nightmare fuel. He was aware of Joe's temper and knew he was a monster, but to watch him go full caveman on Mosser like that, beating his head to a pulp with the man's own fake leg?

Goddamn.

Marlin squat-stepped to the rear of the truck and reached over the side, removing the post digger wedge as quietly as he could, but the end of the iron spike bumped the tailgate and pinged across the air in a reedy echo. Joe made no move to acknowledge it, just stood staring at the mess on his driveway and smiling through the blood spatter. Marlin started to make his way to the front of the truck when he saw movement near the edge of the lawn. He looked and saw Lisa standing at the corner of the house, between the shed and the privacy hedge. She stared at the brutal tableau before her, and he heard her gasp from where he hunkered. That sharp intake of breath caused Joe to break from his daze and whirl around to its source.

"Good for you to see this, Lisa. You sent out the fuckin' invitations. You bein' the one done brought it on." Joe kicked the leg on the ground, making the metal hinge clatter loudly against the cement. Lisa shook her head, the tears on her cheeks glistened.

"What'd you do, Joe?" Her voice was shrill and needling.

"Show'd 'em I ain't the one, babe. Not the one to fuck with. At all. Ever." He laughed and it was clotted with madness.

He took another step towards his wife and Marlin saw a sliver of a chance to make his move. He took a few low jogging steps into the yard before he stopped, metal spike raised like a spear, back over head and shoulder, ready to fly.

"Lisa, down!" he yelled, his underused voice crinkling like wrapping paper. He threw the pole and Joe turned at the sound of Marlin's yelling. The night went silent in that moment, the only sound the slight whistle of the opportune javelin as it sailed towards its mark. Joe never saw it against the dark before it bore through his back, the wedged end taking most of his lung out through a hole in his chest. He stood, teetering for a long minute before he started to fall, but didn't. Not quite. The spike acted like a kickstand and held his sagging body almost upright. Bent at the knees but not falling. Lisa screamed and rushed to her husband. Marlin stood, shaking, and quietly crying.

What else was I to do?

He found a slight distraction in the gray cat that was licking blood from the hand of Mosser's corpse. Marlin looked up at the moon and swore he saw a face in it, just before he hit the ground.

— 44 —

"Marlin?"

The voice was static. Breaking apart. He felt a small hand rubbing his cheek. He willed his eyes to open and looked into the red face of Lisa. Her cheeks coated in tears and a hand-shaped welt on her cheek.

"Oh, Marlin. What a mess." Lisa helped him to sit upright. Seeing the scene again, he nearly fainted a second time.

"Lisa. I never meant to kill nobody. I had no design to, until I saw what he did to them and saw him coming for you."

Her hand found his, fingers knotting like briar.

"I know," she said.

"But you're free now. And safe. "

They sat quiet for a few minutes before Marlin struggled to stand. He leaned back and pulled Lisa up, she smiled wearily at him as she rose, and he saw her arm snake out and he closed his eyes welcoming the incoming embrace.

Instead, there came a sharp pain in his side. Burning beneath rib and lung. Marlin hissed and opened his eyes to see Lisa holding a screwdriver in her hand.

"What?" was all he could manage, his head swimming from the confusion and fresh pain.

"You sweet idiot. All I wanted was you to break the leash for me. Dead or in jail, I didn't care. I just wanted no Joe. And bless you, Marlin, you did that. But the rest of this mess.... that's just stronger fucking chain! I will never be able to go anywhere. I'll be tied here until the cops are done sifting and snooping, and then no matter where I go, I'll be penned behind the invisible fence of gossip and dirty looks. Idle talk and judgement. You told Mosser and this is the bomb crater." She smiled and looked at the screwdriver in her hand, at the red dripping from the tip onto her lawn. She smiled and tilted her head like a pageant queen.

"That was the screwdriver Wade stabbed Joe with. Then Joe killed Wade and Mosser then you pegged Joe and came for me, but Joe nipped you before he kicked it." Lisa looked at her husband and just as quickly back to Marlin.

"I really ought to be grateful, I mean you did what I wanted but the extra is too much. Now, you made yourself a string that needs to be snipped or I'm never gonna be able to fly."

"But Lisa…I love you. I wanted to…"

"Think I wasn't aware of that? Marlin, I counted on that. I'm sorry…."

As Marlin fell to the pavement, Lisa slid the tool from his torso and slipped it into her pocket. She kissed her fingertips and touched them to his lips, before she disappeared into the darkness at the end of the driveway, thinking the whole time how thankful she was Joe built their house in the boonies.

— 45 —

Back of an envelope, Found in Notebook #65, Black Sharpie:
"Death is a ridiculous symphony. Bones and blood and breath and wish and why all whirling under the tongue of the living. Tasting of egg and Sepsis. Eternity is a feast for one."

— 46 —

Something sandy touched his cheek and Marlin opened a weak eye to see the infantile face before his.

"Baby brother."

"Oh, Merle…oh, what a mess."

"I know, I know. But let's not talk about that now. We've got always for that."

Marlin nodded as he used all his will to sit up, and then stand. His ribs throbbed. Thick blood had soaked the entirety of the left side of his flannel. He held a hand against the wound and winced. Merle just watched and when his brother was standing steadier, followed him to the truck.

"I need to get home." Marlin whispered as he struggled to get the truck in gear with the shifter slipping from his gory hand.

"Yes," was the cat's reply as it sat on the passenger seat and watched the scenery begin to move outside the window, while the moon seemed stuck in place.

— 47 —

The trailer door squeaked when he opened it. He paused and heard the theme from *The Rockford Files* at low volume and couldn't help but smile. Mama loved her old shows. Merle was already ahead of him, and Marlin hobbled to catch up. He rounded the corner into the living room and his stomach dropped like a lead sinker in brackish water.

Mama was laying in her chair, eyes barely open and her breathing coming rabbit fast. Her hair and skin were glistening with sweat and the room smelled different. He touched her cheek and leaned in close.

"Oh, Mama. I'm here."

She opened her eyes a bit wider but not without great effort.

"Honey, I knew you'd be here soon. I held on for you, Son." Her hand found his and squeezed it hard enough he could feel all the bones of her fingers.

"I am here, Mama. I am. You just close your eyes and hold on; I have something for you."

She nodded wearily and her eyes shut. Her breathing stayed ragged and fast, but she was asleep. Marlin looked at his brother and the cat said nothing, just nodded. The man with the hole in his side pulled the blanket around his mother's skeletal form and lifted her from the chair. He carried her out into the night.

— 48 —

"You remember that time I asked you about Dad? I asked you if he was a good man." Marlin's breath was a huffing thing. It' was wet and ragged. "You told me that story about the boat and the lake…"

The words were getting heavy as bricks, the loss of blood and the effort of carrying this small woman through the woods was conspiring against him. With every step over tree root and stone, he grew more exhausted.

Dying sure is hard work.

"Mama, something happened tonight. And I know I did something terrible, but for a good reason. I thought, why do things always seem so much simpler than they ever are?"

"Marlin…what are you on about?" Her voice was small and timid.

"Mama."

"Where are we and why are you carrying me like a baby?"

Marlin breathed heavier as he made his way up the last hill before the small field between the woods.

"Marlin!" She tried to sound stern, but the power was gone. Marlin just hugged her closer and hissed out painful breaths with every footfall.

"You're soaking wet, boy." The woman worked a hand free, weakly, and looked at it in the bright moonlight.

"My God, you're bleeding."

"Never stopped…here we are, Mama."

He topped the hill and he stopped and lowered his arms enough for his mother to see her gift.

— 49 —

The bottom of the hill spread out into a clearing about the size of a football field. It was relatively flat and devoid of much brush and bramble. The ground below them twinkled in the starlight, the dancing reflection in the dozens of mirrors that covered the earth. Various shapes and sizes. Positioned in the middle of them was a small boat. An old aluminum affair. The sky above and below it, like heaven's cradling hands.

The dying woman poked her head up above the blanket, and as her tired eyes took in what was before them, she gasped and smiled as big as she could manage.

"Oh My." was all she managed.

Marlin held her close and started slowly down.

— 50 —

Marlin stepped into the boat, his boots clunking on the aluminum bottom. He slowly put his mother down on the floor so she could lean back against the seat. He then eased himself down on the seat adjacent. He groaned and the moon threw a spotlight on the gruesome stain that took up his left side.

"What have you done?" Mama whispered. Her breathing was much faster, and her eyes were wild. The pain must have been fierce.

"Nothing good. Nothing on purpose." He paused and looked at the reflection of the stars and moon in all the mirrors placed around the boat. He had created a lake of reflective glass.

She took his hand and held it to her heart. He felt it racing and closed his eyes. He kept them closed and felt it begin to slow.

"Mama."

"Yeah?"

"I love you."

"I love you too, Son."

"I think I'm dying"

"Don't talk foolish."

She managed to raise her head and look out at the twinkling in the glass on the ground.

"Thank you for this. You gave me back one of the best memories I ever had."

"You're welcome." Marlin leaned forward to lay his head on his mother's chest. Her heart slowed from its spastic racing to a slow tattoo.

He slid back and slumped in his seat, his chest rising slow and her hand in his until his chest stopped moving at all. His Mama watched the moon and wept for her son until her heart stopped as well. The moon and stars reflecting in her open eyes as well as the lake of mirrors.

The morning sun was bright and cheerful, and it poked its thick fingers into the dark spaces around the county.

The police had arrived late, coming from two towns over, after being called to the grisly scene at Joe's. They had gone to the Stains residence to ask some questions about Sorrel when they found the blood on the porch and in the house. They followed the red trail over the bank behind the trailer and to the gulley beyond. The officers would go on to report that it had beaten anything they had ever seen before. An emaciated woman and her son both dead, in an old boat on dry land surrounded by mirrors.

The silver-backed glass peppered with small bloody paw prints.

— 52 —

Back of an envelope left on Miriam Stains counter, pencil:
"Your mother's heart is the first drum you hear…there's magic in that."

SNARL

Acknowledgements

I hate this part. I always fret so hard over forgetting people that I usually end up listing some folks more than once. So lemme give it another go…and if you aren't listed don't feel bad. I still love you…with all my calloused heart,

Thanks to Jeremy Wagner, Steve Wands, Anna Kubik, and Kristy Baptist for taking me under their black wings at Dead Sky.

Thanks to my Mama and baby brother. My lovely wife and sons. Cousins and uncles and aunts…even if we never speak. I love you all. --see also, work family.

Thanks to Chad Lutzke, Bob Ford, Chris Enterline, Waylon Glunt, Lori Lane, Taniele Fastnacht, Steve Wynne, Justin Lutz, Sadie Hartman, Alan Baxter, Jacob Haddon, Ken Wood, John Skipp, Bracken MacLeod, Mercedes Yardley, Shawn Macomber, Patrick Freivald, Sam W. Anderson, Kelli Owen, James Newman, Todd Keisling, Mark Allan Gunnells, Craig Metcalf, Kevin Lucia, Ronald Malfi, Kenneth Cain, Somer Canon, Kris Triana, Brian Keene, Mary SanGiovanni, Dave Thomas and Deena, Mark Matthews, John Foster, Michael Wehunt, Matthew Bartlett, Wes Southard and Katie, Robert Moore, Wendy Deeley, Bill Lengeman III, Autumn Christian, Ron Davis, Ronald Kelly, Philip Fracassi, Josh Malerman, Ron Dickie, Jarod Barbee, and Gary McMahon.

Special thanks to the inspirators--Stephen Graham Jones, Steve Rasnic Tem, S.A. Cosby, Joe Lansdale, Aaron Dries, John Prine, Jack Ketchum, Billy Joe Shaver, Ron Rash and Ray Bradbury.

And thank YOU!

Also by John Boden

Dominoes

Jedi Summer

Spungunion

Walk The Darkness Down

Detritus in Love (With Mercedes M. Yardley)

Out Behind The Barn (With Chad Lutzke)

Rattlesnake Kisses (With Robert Ford)

Cattywampus (With Robert Ford)

Dark Tide Book I: Wounds To Wishes—Tales Of Mystery And Melancholy (With Chad Lutzke and Robert Ford)

About the author

John Boden lives with his beautiful wife and two sons, in a house sweetly haunted by the ghost of a beautician named, Darlene. He likes collecting lots of things and won't usually shut up about it. His writing is fairly well received and has been called unique of style. His work has been published in the form of stories in several anthologies and as novellas. He plays well with others as is evidenced by collaborative works with Mercedes M. Yardley, Bracken MacLeod, Kurt Newton, Brian Rosenberger, Chad Lutzke and Robert Ford.

He's easy to track down either on Facebook or Twitter (JohnBoden1970).